To Laika

Atheneum Books for Young Readers

An imprint of Simon & Schuster Children's Publishing Division

1230 Avenue of the Americas, New York, New York 10020

Copyright © 2005 by Marjorie Priceman

Book design by Jessica Sonkin

The text for this book is set in Celestia Antiqua.

Manufactured in Mexico

10 9 8 7 6 5 4 3 2

Library of Congress Cataloging-in-Publication Data

Priceman, Marjorie.

Hot air : the (mostly) true story of the first hot-air balloon ride / Marjorie Priceman.— 1st ed.

p. cm.

ISBN 0-689-82642-7

1. Balloon ascensions—France—Versailles—History. 2. Montgolfier, Jacques-Etienne, 1745–1799.

3. Montgolfier, Joseph-Michel, 1740–1810. I. Title.

TL620.M66P75 2005

629.133'22'0929—dc22

2004014743

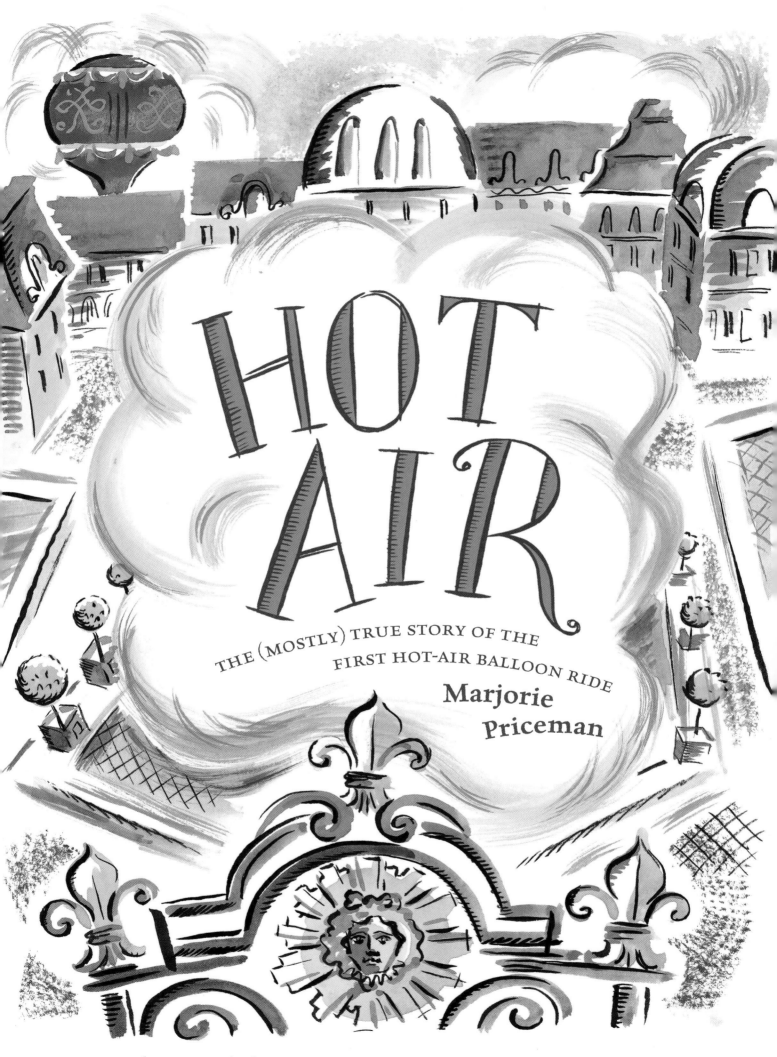

HOT AIR

THE (MOSTLY) TRUE STORY OF THE FIRST HOT-AIR BALLOON RIDE

Marjorie Priceman

Atheneum Books for Young Readers • New York • London • Toronto • Sydney

SEPTEMBER 19, 1783.

Thousands of people have come to watch an incredible experiment at the palace of Versailles in France.

Ah, Versailles! 700 rooms! 67 staircases! 15 fountains! 2,000 acres of manicured gardens! Too many chandeliers, paintings, and gold bathtubs to count!

But enough about that.

What a crowd has assembled! Scientists, schoolchildren, opera singers, and architects. Noblemen, farmers, and one famous pastry chef. Even the American ambassador, Benjamin Franklin, is here. And, of course, King Louis XVI and Queen Marie Antoinette.

But enough about them.

The demonstration is about to begin! After months of work and many sleepless nights, the amateur inventors Joseph and Etienne Montgolfier are ready to test an exciting new kind of transportation—the hot-air balloon.

So, never mind the important people and splendid surroundings. Pay no attention to that little dog or that lady with the towering hairdo.

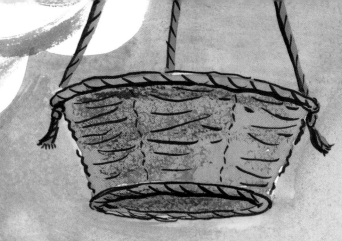

Look, instead, at the basket attached by slender ropes to the balloon now rising high above the crowd.

Inside that basket are ballooning's first brave passengers. . . .

A duck,
a sheep,
and a rooster.

This is

their

story.

Baaaaa!

QUACK QUACK QUACK

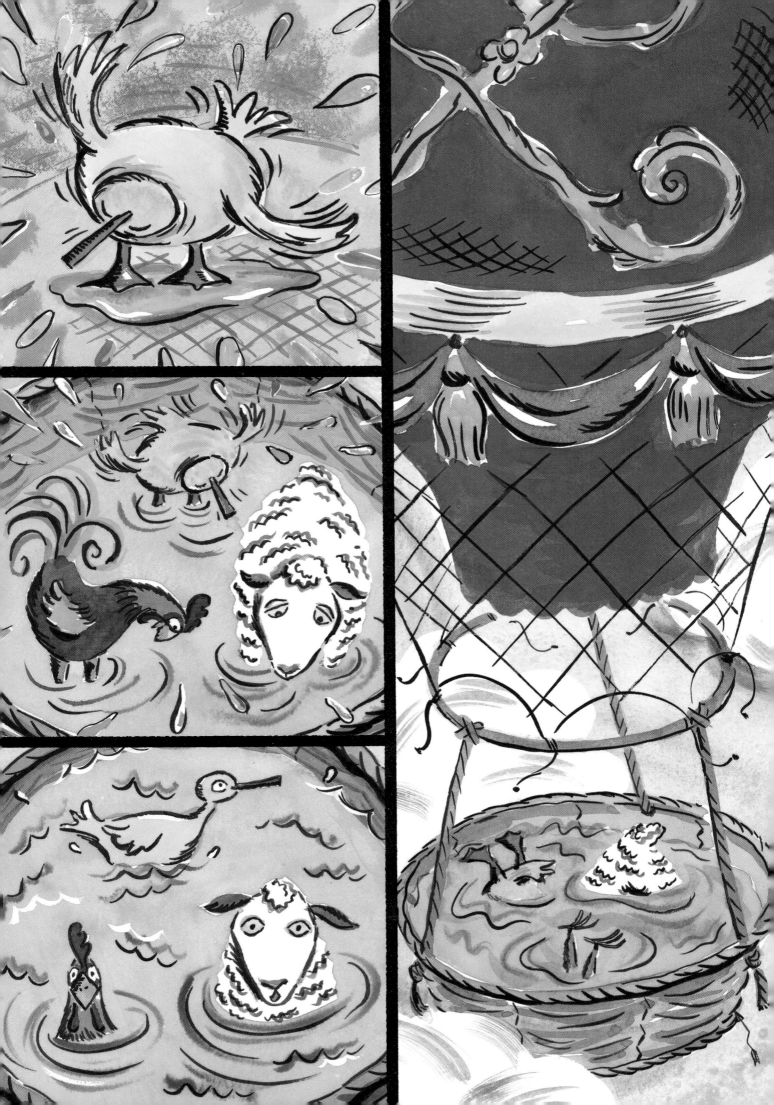

POP!

Happiness and joy! An historic event! Our brave aviators, who have touched down in the woods at Vaucresson, are found in fine fluff and feather and carried back to Versailles. There they are greeted with flowers, song, and better food than usual.

But enough about that.

You may be wondering, did this really happen? Well, yes—sort of. The Montgolfiers were real people who are considered the inventors of the hot-air balloon and the fathers of aviation. The September 19, 1783, balloon flight with barnyard animal passengers is a matter of historical record. But the details of the flight may or may not be true. The author heard this part of the story from a duck, who heard it from a sheep, who heard it from a rooster a long, long time ago.

A BRIEF HISTORY OF MONTGOLFIERS' BALLOONS

NOVEMBER 1782—AVIGNON, FRANCE

Joseph Montgolfier ran his family's paper company, but at heart he was a dreamer and inventor. One evening he watched smoke from the fire carry bits of ash up the chimney, and he wondered: Can smoke lift other objects?*

Using materials at hand, he made a box by stretching fabric on a thin wooden frame, leaving an opening at the bottom. He then lit some twists of paper and held them at the opening, filling the box with hot, smoky air. Much to his delight, the contraption lifted off the table and floated up to the ceiling.

DECEMBER 14, 1782—ANNONAY

Together the Montgolfier brothers repeated the experiment outdoors with a model three times the size of the original. It floated away, landing in a distant field.

JUNE 4, 1783—ANNONAY

A public exhibition of the new larger and rounder device. To combat the cool, wet weather, a brazier was attached to the balloon. On landing, the brazier tipped and set the balloon on fire. The flight was a great success nonetheless and news reached Paris. The Academy of Science invited the Montgolfiers to demonstrate their invention for the king at Versailles.